HOLDEN PUBLIC LIBRARY

A40600192817

P9-ASB-109

THE DAMON MEMORIAL

JJ
KRA
Kraus, Robert

Come out and play, little
mouse   HOLDEN

WITHDRAWN FROM LIBRARY

GALE FREE LIBRARY
Holden, Massachusetts

NOV 1 1987

Come Out and Play,

Little Mouse

by **Robert Kraus**

pictures by **Jose Aruego**
and **Ariane Dewey**

Greenwillow Books, New York

Text copyright © 1987 by Robert Kraus
Illustrations copyright © 1987 by Jose Aruego and Ariane Dewey
All rights reserved. No part of this book may be reproduced or
utilized in any form or by any means, electronic or mechanical,
including photocopying, recording or by any information storage
and retrieval system, without permission in writing from the
Publisher, Greenwillow Books, a division of William Morrow
& Company, Inc., 105 Madison Avenue, New York, N.Y. 10016.
Printed in the United States of America
First Edition 10 9 8 7 6 5 4 3 2 1

The artwork was prepared as black pen-and-ink
line drawings which were combined with full-color
paintings. The typeface is Avant Garde Gothic.

Library of Congress Cataloging-in-Publication Data

Kraus, Robert, (date)
Come out and play, little mouse.
Summary: Little mouse is busy helping his family five days
of the week, but he gets to play with them on weekends.
[1. Mice—Fiction. 2. Days—Fiction] I. Aruego, Jose, ill.
II. Dewey, Ariane, ill. III. Title.
PZ7.K868Co 1987 [E] 85-30198
ISBN 0-688-05837-X ISBN 0-688-05838-8 (lib. bdg.)

For Parker
—R. K.

For Juan
—J. A. and A. D.

MONDAY

Come out and play,
little mouse.

I can't play today.
I'm going shopping with my mother.
Ask me tomorrow.

TUESDAY

Come out and play,
little mouse.

I can't play today.
I've got to help my father
paint the kitchen.
Ask me tomorrow.

WEDNESDAY

Come out and play,
little mouse.

I can't play today.
I've got to help my sister
do the laundry.
Ask me tomorrow.

THURSDAY

Come out and play,
little mouse.

I can't play today.
I've got to help my little brother
with his homework.
Ask me tomorrow.

FRIDAY

Come out and play,
little mouse.

I can't play today.
I've got to clean my room.
Ask me tomorrow.

SATURDAY

Come out and play,
little mouse.

My big brother's busy,
but I'll play with you.

Let's play hide and seek,

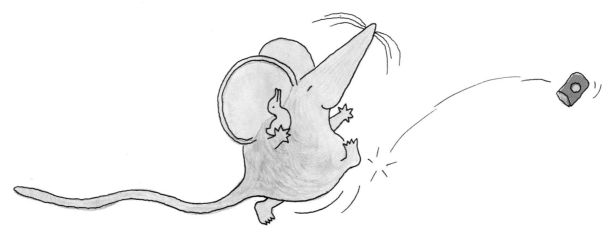

let's play kick the can,

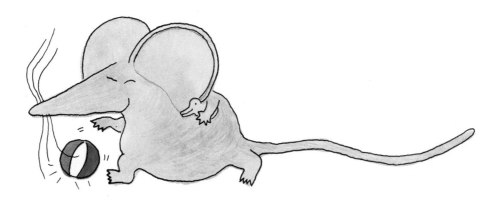

let's play ball,

let's play cards,

let's play jacks,

let's play hopscotch.

NO! LET'S PLAY CAT AND MOUSE.

You run, I catch you.

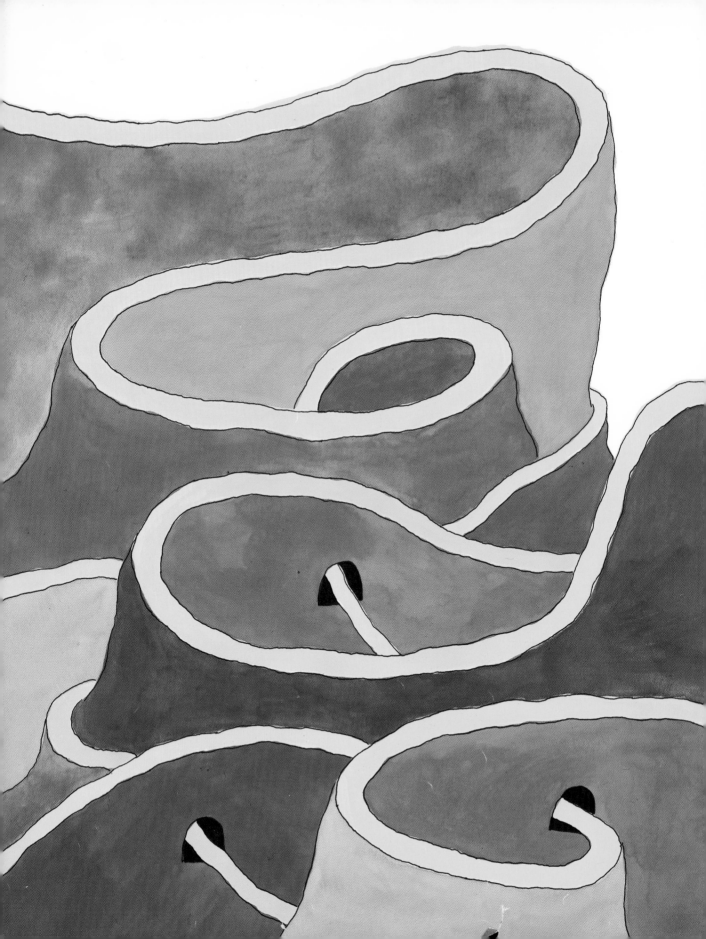

NO, IT'S NOT!
LET'S PLAY DOG AND CAT.

Thank you, dog.

I'm not a dog!
I'm your big brother.

SUNDAY

Come out and play,
little mice.

We can't play today.

We're playing with our family.